To Georgia and Kitty

No Such Thing

ELLA BAILEY

FLYING EYE BOOKS

LONDON - NEW YORK

One cool day in late October
Georgia noticed something weird.

Objects would move around the house,

and sometimes they even disappeared.

Now some people may have wondered (especially at this time of year),
was this the work of something spooky?

But not clever Georgia here!

When snacks were stolen from the fridge

this savvy sleuth knew who,

and when a china vase was smashed she guessed who did that, too.

She presumed to know who pinched her socks so she had none to wear,

and she saw who swiped her coloured crayons –
the evidence was there!

Georgia suspected who snatched her sheets whilst hanging out to dry,

she also spied the pumpkin thief
hiding somewhere nearby.

When the house was strewn with webs in every corner, all around,

the culprit was just over there,
scuttling away along the ground!

With one look out of the window she deduced who pilfered her broom!

Luckily Georgia had a spare that she could use with her costume.

Even shadows and strange noises she noticed late at night,

could be explained away simply
by using a torch light.

These little thieves and mischief makers could all somehow be reasoned
– not all, but certainly most –

because surely,
absolutely,
unquestionably,
we all know...

...there's just no such thing as ghosts!

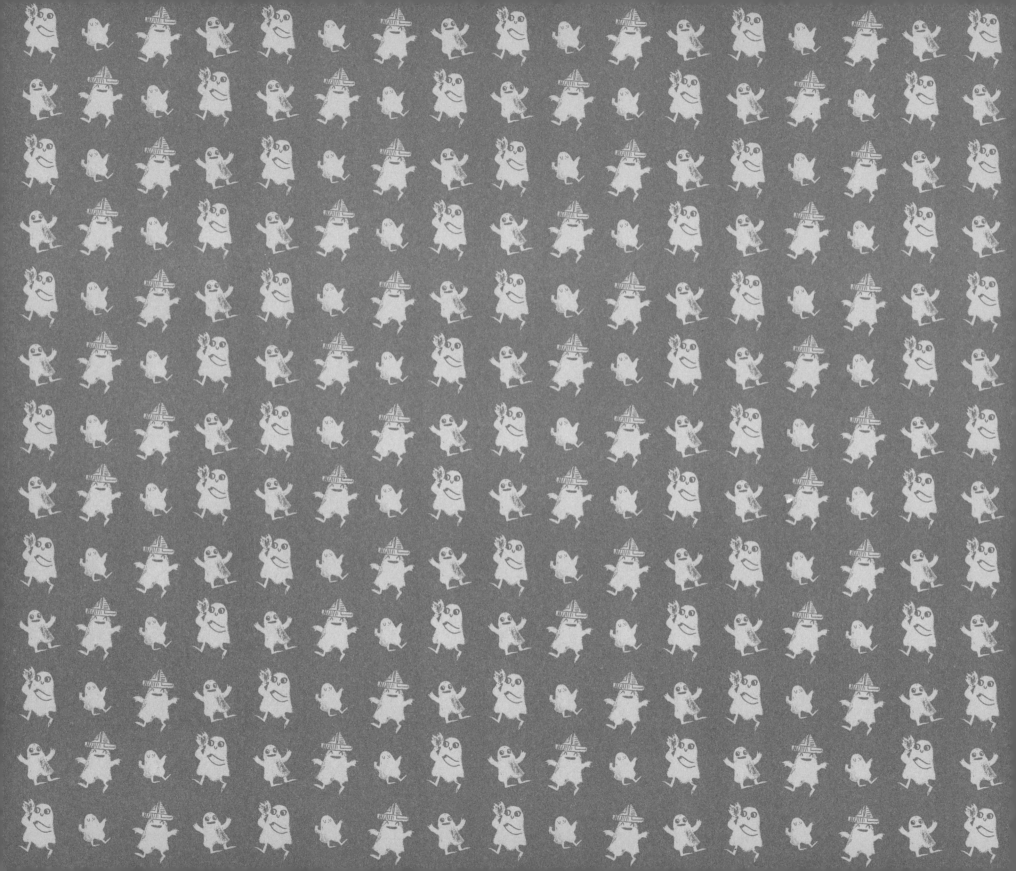